# lauren child

# My wobbly tooth must NOT ever NEVER fall out

PUFFIN

Text based on script written by Samantha Hill

Illustrations from the TV animation

produced by Tiger Aspect

PUFFIN BOOKS
Published by the Penguin Group, London, New York, Australia,
Canada, India, Ireland, New Zealand and South Africa
Penguin Books Ltd, Registered Offices: 80 Strand, London WC2R 0RL, England

puffinbooks.com

First published 2006
Published in this edition 2007
1 3 5 7 9 10 8 6 4 2
Text and illustrations copyright © Lauren Child/Tiger Aspect Productions Limited, 2006
The Charlie and Lola logo is a trademark of Lauren Child
All rights reserved
The moral right of the author/illustrator has been asserted
Made and printed in China
ISBN: 978-0-141-50127-7

Original recording © Tiger Aspect Productions Limited, 2006
Copyright in this recording © Penguin Books, 2007
All rights reserved
This edition manufactured and distributed by Penguin Books Ltd 2007

I have this little sister Lola.
  She is small and very funny.
This week she got her
    first ever wobbly tooth.

Lola says,
    "I do not ever NEVER want
    my wobbly tooth to fall out."

Marv says, "When I had my first wobbly tooth,
        I nearly swallowed it.
    Luckily I was eating a toffee...
            and my tooth got stuck in it!"

I say, "Once I headed a football
and my wobbly tooth just flew out
of my mouth!"

"But I do not ever NEVER
want my wobbly tooth
to fall out," says Lola.

Marv says, "Why don't
you want it to fall out?"

"I just need to keep completely
all my teeth," says Lola.

And I say, "Those are just your baby teeth
and they are meant to
get wobbly and fall out.
Then you will get new teeth – and
they are your grown-up ones."

"It's like mooses," I say. "Mooses' antlers
**fall off** and then they get **new** ones which are
better and **stronger**."

"But I am **not** a moose!
It's my **wobbly tooth** and
I want to **keep** it... **wobbly**," says Lola.

Later Lotta comes over to play with Lola.
    "Lola, Lola!"

Lola says,
"What is it, Lotta? What is it?"
And Lotta says,
    "My tooth fell out!"

"What did you get?"
says Marv.

"What do you mean, what did you get?" says Lola.
And Lotta says,
"Well, the tooth fairy came and..."
"Who is the tooth fairy?!" says Lola.

"Well, the tooth fairy is the tooth fairy...
   I lost my wobbly tooth, I put it under my pillow,
  and then in the middle of the night
the tooth fairy came and then I got
  a coin," says Lotta.
   "And in the morning
I bought this for
   the farm.
It's a
   chicken!"

Lola says,

"I didn't know there was a special fairy who gives you presents when your teeth fall out! Why didn't somebody tell me this before?

"My wobbly tooth must completely
come out! Now!"

Lotta says,
    "When your tooth falls out,
what are you going to get?
    We need a horse and a sheep...
and a cow."

    And Lola says,
        "I'm going to get
            a giraffe."

"Do you get giraffes on a farm?"
says Lotta.

And Lola says,
"Yes, you absolutely do, Lotta...

"... but how do I get my wobbly tooth to fall out?"

And Lotta says, "Does it feel wobbly enough?"

Lola says, "I think it's almost nearly about to come out..."

And Lotta says, "You have to keep wobbling it."

Marv says,
"Do you want me to twist it?"
"No, Marv!" says Lola. "Mum said
absolutely no twisting!"
And I say, "Keep wobbling, Lola."

"I've been **wobbling** it for ages," she says. "It's still not coming **out**.

I don't think it's **ever** going to **come out**."

Then she squeals,
"Aaagh!

It's out!
My wobbly tooth
is really out!
And now I can get my giraffe!"

Lotta says,
    "You have to put it under your pillow
in the very, very middle.
        You must go to bed early,
            and you must fall asleep quickly,
    or the tooth fairy won't come."

    Lola says, "Yes. Because I really want
                    my giraffe."

"I really want the giraffe too!" says Lotta.

"When you come over tomorrow,"
      says Lola, "I can have my giraffe
and you can bring your chicken
            and they can be friends."

"Yes, yes, yes!" says Lotta.
      "Bye, Lola!"

At bedtime Lola says,
   "Charlie, I'm just going to wash
my **tooth** and make it **shiny** and **clean**.
   And then I...

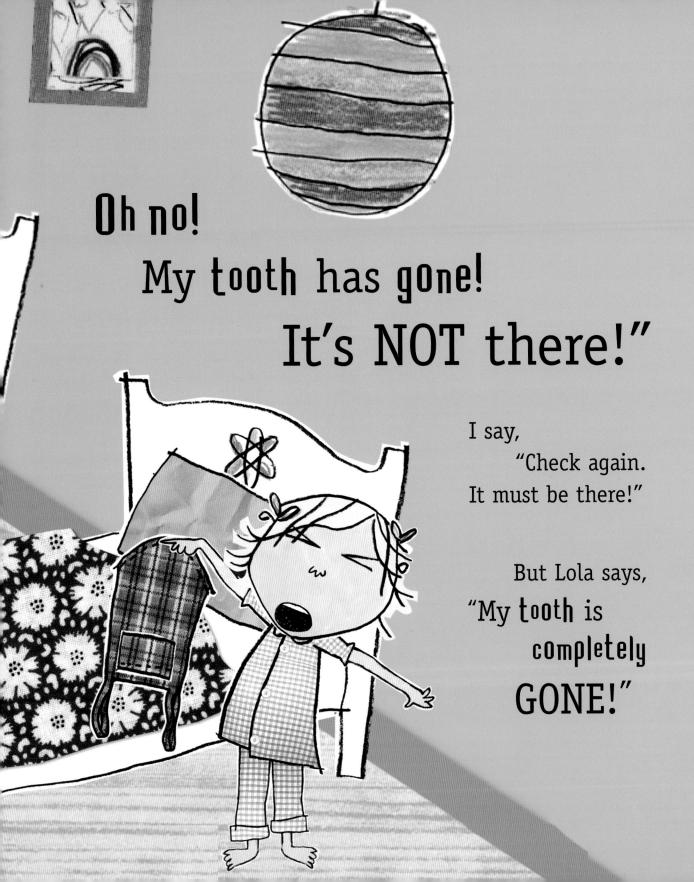

Oh no!
My tooth has gone!
It's NOT there!"

I say,
"Check again.
It must be there!"

But Lola says,
"My tooth is
completely
GONE!"

I say,
"It must be somewhere!"

So we
start
searching
everywhere.

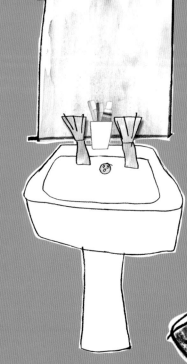

We look in the sink,

and

under
the
beds,

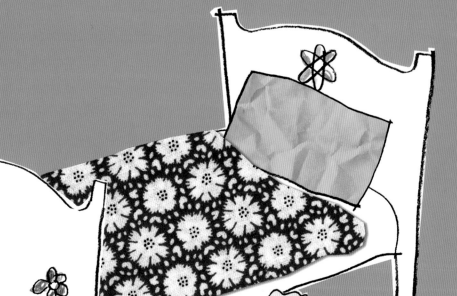

on     the     floor,

and

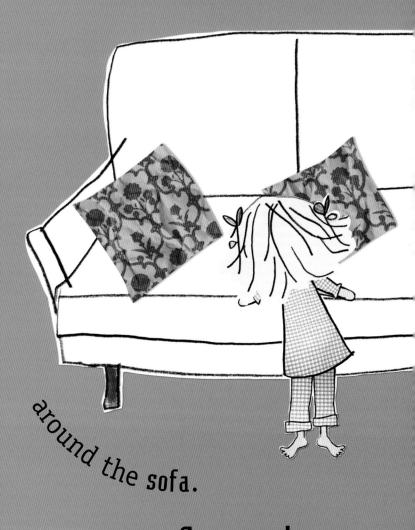

around the sofa.

Everywhere.

Then I have a really good idea.

"If you go to sleep and dream really
happy dreams, you will **smile**.
And then the **tooth fairy** will see
the **gap** in your **teeth**,
and she'll know you really did
lose your **tooth!**"

So Lola goes to bed.

"Really happy dreams.
Really happy dreams. Really happy..."

In the morning
Lola looks **under** the very
middle of her pillow.

She says,

"Charlie! The tooth fairy did come!
Look! Hurry, hurry, Charlie,
I need to get a giraffe!"

When Lotta comes to play with Lola she says,
    "What's your **giraffe** called?"
Lola says, "**Giraffe**. And what about your **chicken**?"
    Lotta says, "It's called **Chicken**!"
"Oh **look!** I think they're **friends**," says Lola.

Then Lola says, "Maybe Giraffe and Chicken
would like to meet Mr Goat?
Oh, we don't have a goat."
"How will we get a goat?" says Lotta.
"We need more wobbly teeth!" says Lola.
"Have you got any more wobbly teeth?"

Lotta says, "No."
"What about this one?" says Lola.
"No," says Lotta.
Lola says, "Try that one.
This one? This one? This one..."